Tim A...

Bagpipes
Beasties
and Bogles

This is a story from Scotland long ago.

If you trudged a twisty track,
and rambled in the rain.
If you jumped a thistle thicket,
and splashed across a stream.
If you climbed a heather hill,
and spied a secret glen.
There you would find,
in a sunny house of stone,
lived Charlie McCandlewick.

He did not have many visitors.

Most days Charlie worked in his beautiful garden.
He grew raspberries and rhubarb, potatoes and porridge spoons.

Charlie McCandlewick was a nightsweep.
But wait, cheery cherub, before you rush off for hot chocolate
and a handful of Happy Giant butter biscuits, tighten your
pyjamas, because...

Charlie McCandlewick did not sweep CHIMNEYS.
He did not sing and dance about sweeping chimneys.
It was the bogle creatures of the night that he swept away.
All of the things that knock and bump, shuffle, shift, hiss
and whisper in your house at night.

The scratching and skittering in the old cupboard is not a
friendly rabbit sewing trousers, it is not a cheerful mouse
saving crumbs for the winter.

It is a *SOMETHING* and it's IN YOUR ROOM.

People in farms and villages, in castles and cottages, would send for old Charlie. "Something is knocking at night," they told him. "We're frightened, Charlie," said the children.

"A bogle has blackened our bread and puggled our porridge," they told him.

"What a fuss," you might say, "about a few bumps in the night."
But, remember…

Long ago in Charlie McCandlewick's time there was NO electricity, NO television, NO telephones, NO teddy bears. It was a dark and dingy time.

Now be brave and read on.

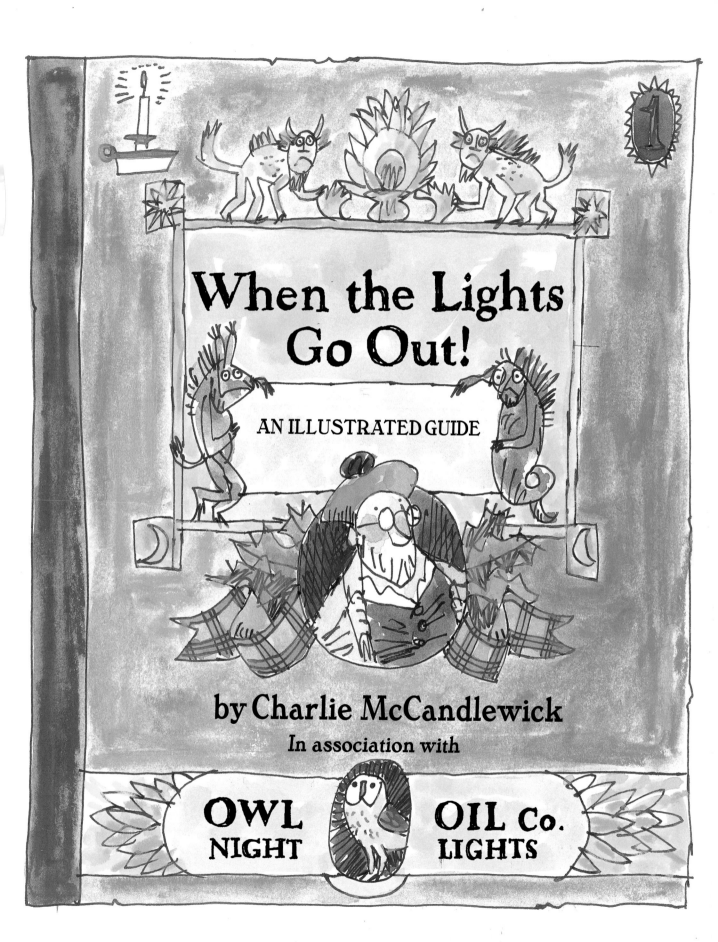

When the Lights Go Out!

AN ILLUSTRATED GUIDE

by Charlie McCandlewick

In association with

OWL
NIGHT

OIL Co.
LIGHTS

A Fankle twists your clothes into terrible knots.

Coughing Croakies flap about in cupboards.

Squeakers are creatures that live on dark stairs.

A Grunnoch tries on your clothes in the night. Underpants will be inside-out and socks lost.

Skelpies live under the floor.
They eat fluff and crumbs.

Nippers and Nabbers wait under your bed for a foot to appear.

A greedy Gurdle will eat your last piece of bread or the last chocolate in the box.

Charlie knew what to do.

VOLCANO BRAND
leather gloves

Cheese & pickle
sandwich

THE WOLF & WILDCAT CO.
No.8 Willowtwist rope

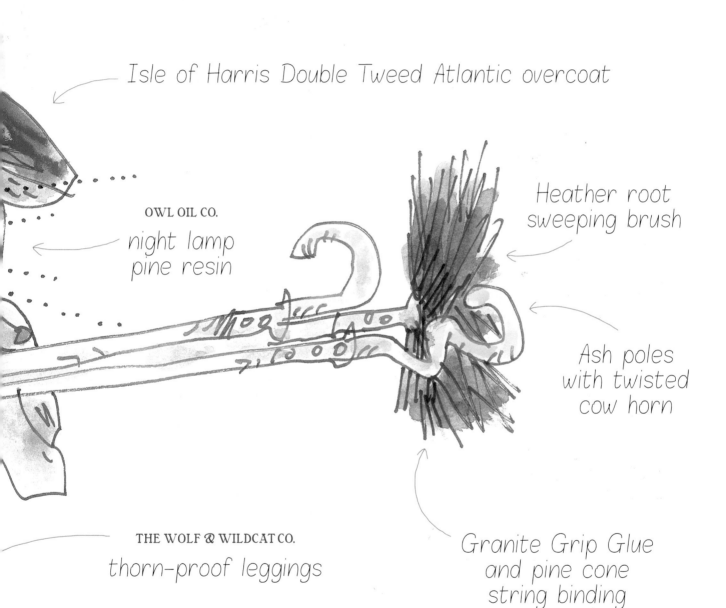

Bags made from best Scottish thistle cloth
ISLE OF SKYE THISTLE CLOTH CO. EST. 1297

Isle of Harris Double Tweed Atlantic overcoat

OWL OIL CO.
night lamp
pine resin

Heather root
sweeping brush

Ash poles
with twisted
cow horn

THE WOLF & WILDCAT CO.
thorn-proof leggings

Granite Grip Glue
and pine cone
string binding

Boots made in Scotland
THE SILENT SQUIRREL CO. SINCE 1745

With VOLCANO BRAND gloves he grabbed
the Nippers and Nabbers that goggled
in the gloom beneath a bed.

He crept with SILENT SQUIRREL
boots and caught the Skelpies
that scuttered under
farmhouse floors.

With his heather root brush,
he swept away the shadows
and shapes on twisting stairs.

With an OWL OIL lamp he lured wailing Whigmaleeries.

Charlie caught creatures
that clacked on claws...

And whinged at windows…

And muttered at midnight.

He put all of these creatures into special bags made from thistle cloth.

The bogle creatures did not like being caught and jumbled together in a bag, so they began to screech.

THEY BIT AND SPIT

THEY GROWLED AND HOWLED

THEY WAILED AND FLAILED

THEY MOANED AND GROANED

THEY FLAPPED AND FLUTTERED

THEY THRASHED AND

CRASHED AND

GNASHED THEIR TEETH

They cried and tried to escape
but could not…

...so they went to sleep.

Charlie was paid for his nightsweeping. He packed up his tools, gathered up the thistle cloth bags and walked home for breakfast.

You might now be worrying about Nippers and Nabbers under your bed. You might be thinking, "I must have some Silent Squirrel boots." But wait – this is not the end of the story.

After a breakfast of porridge and raspberries, Charlie walked up to the windy wood.

He cut a bundle of pine and soaked it in a barrel filled with a secret mixture of golden barley and six kinds of rain.

He shaped and drilled the pine into pipes. He rubbed each pipe with duck oil, and whipped them together with wildcat whiskers.

Charlie used Granite Grip Glue to join the pipes to one of the thistle cloth bags.

What do you think Charlie was making?

Charlie McCandlewick made bagpipes of course!

This is how bagpipes work

1. The piper blows into the thistle cloth bag and gives it a good slap.

2. The creatures inside wake up and begin to wail.

3. The piper blows hard into the bag and gives it a squeeze.

4. Inside the bag the creatures fight and flap, they screech and skirl, they wail and drone.

5. The piper moves his fingers up and down the chanter just to keep them warm.

6. The piper must keep blowing and squeezing and walking and looking important.

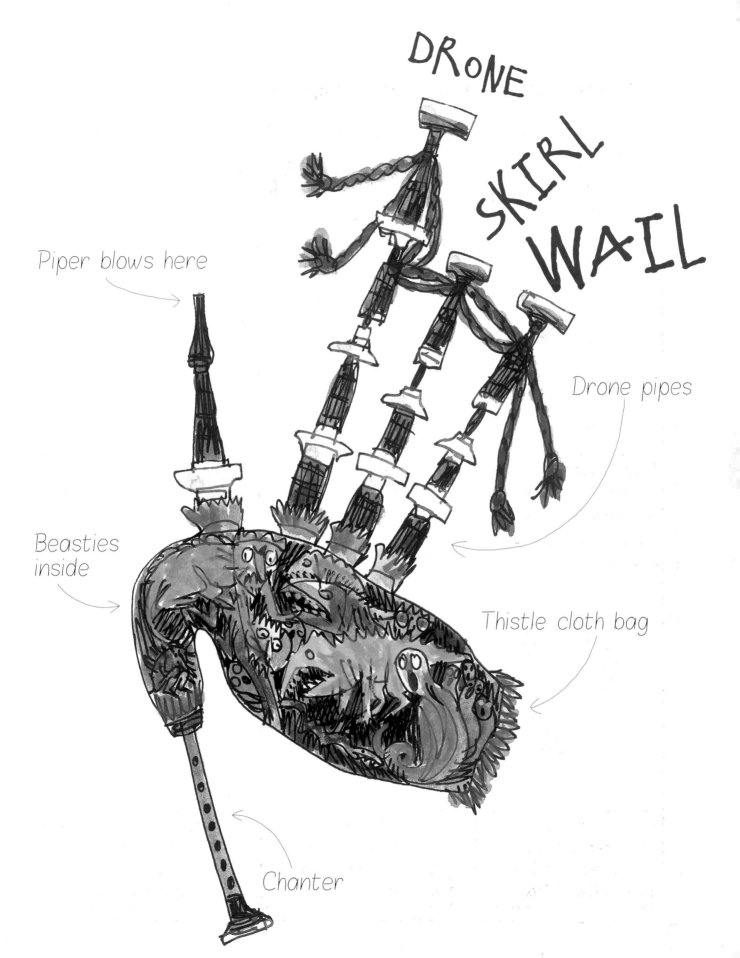

DRONE

SKIRL

WAIL

Piper blows here

Drone pipes

Beasties inside

Thistle cloth bag

Chanter

Thanks to Charlie McCandlewick, Scottish bagpipes are the best and most famous in the world.
The music of the bagpipes can make you feel proud and sad.
You might dance over sharp swords, or buy a kilt and stride about like a great chieftain.
You might want to grow a big red beard.

Remember, if you ever learn to play, that bagpipes are alive.
They sometimes need a drink and a crust of bread to eat.

BUT, take care! You must never ever, for any reason, open the thistle cloth bag and look inside…